Bad Cat

by Tracy-Lee McGuinness-Kelly

 LITTLE, BROWN AND COMPANY

New York ~ An AOL Time Warner Company

First Edition

Library of Congress Cataloging-in-Publication Data

McGuinness, Tracy.
   Bad Cat / by Tracy-Lee McGuinness-Kelly. — 1st ed.
      p. cm.
Summary: Bad Cat plays a lot of tricks that turn out all right in the end.
ISBN 0-316-60584-0
  [1. Cats—Fiction. 2. Behavior—Fiction.] I. Title.
PZ7.M478563 Bad 2003
[E]—dc21   2002022488

10 9 8 7 6 5 4 3 2 1

TWP

Printed in Singapore

The illustrations for this book were done in Photoshop on a Mac.
The text was set in Sabon, and the display type was created by the artist.

for Roy, Lotie and Charlie

Bad Cat lived in a huge, dirty city. He called it the Big Stinky. He loved to walk around the Big Stinky and look up at the tall buildings that poked through the clouds.

One morning Bad Cat spotted a brick wall with lots of pots of
paint sitting in front of it. He picked up a paintbrush and started
splotching on colors and singing to himself.

Suddenly a booming voice interrupted all the fun. "Hey, you, bad cat! Hey, you, stop that!" Mr. Bigtoe, the owner of the building, came hobbling out, and boy, was he angry! Bad Cat flung his paintbrush in the air and ran away as fast as he could.

Mr. Bigtoe mumbled and grumbled to himself and hobbled over to clean up the mess. Then he looked up at the wall. It was beautiful! "Come back!" he called. "You made my store look so pretty!"

But Bad Cat was already gone.

'I'm a bad cat, bad cat,
said that man,
he thinks I live
in a garbage can!"

Soon Bad Cat was thirsty from all that running. He saw a water fountain and was taking a big drink — *glug, glug, slurrrrp* — when a busy man rushed by him. Bad Cat squirted water, and it knocked off the man's hat.

"Hey, you, bad cat! How dare you do that?" the man yelled. Bad Cat began running as fast as his little legs could carry him.

The busy man wiped the drips of water from his forehead, took off his shoes and smelly socks — *phewwww!* — and rolled up his pant legs. He felt calm and refreshed. "Don't go!" he cried. "You've helped me cool down and relax!"

But Bad Cat was long gone.

"I'm a bad cat, bad cat, that's what they see, they think I'm dangerous, but it's only me!"

Bad Cat stopped running when he saw Mrs. Pooslop in her yard, surrounded by big, blooming flowers. He picked up a pair of clippers and snipped off some of the blossoms.

Suddenly a roaring voice yelled, "Hey, you, bad cat! Don't you do that!" Mr. Pooslop saw the snipped stems and was furious. Bad Cat was on the run again.

Then Mr. Pooslop saw that Bad Cat had given the flowers to Mrs. Pooslop. She was smiling big and wide. Mr. Pooslop hadn't seen her that happy in years.

"Come back!" he shouted. "You've cheered up dear old Hilda!"

But Bad Cat was already on his way.

"I'm a bad cat, bad cat,
that's what they think,
fast cat,
slow cat,
tadpoles in the sink!"

It was late in the day. Bad Cat was getting hungry. He saw a fruit stand and bought a delicious yellow banana.

Bad Cat gobbled it down, and the peel dropped right where Sally Hillybumps and Frederick Wobblebottom were headed toward each other.

Well! Groceries flew up in the air. Eggs cracked, bread rolled, bodies wobbled, turkey was gobbled, potatoes mashed, cherries smashed, tomatoes splattered, fish got battered, milk spilled, and butter patted.

A crowd gathered at this amazing sight. "Hey, you, bad cat! It's terrible you did that!" Bad Cat was so tired by now he couldn't run anymore.

The crowd grabbed him and held him tight. Bad Cat squirmed
with all his might. "Gotcha!" they shouted. Bad Cat knew he was in
terrible trouble. He couldn't even think of a song!

Then Sally piped up over all the racket, "I'm so glad I bumped into you!" Frederick replied, "I'm so glad I bumped into you, too!" Sally and Freddy had slipped on the banana peel and fallen in love.

Everyone heard this and immediately melted. They lifted Bad Cat up onto their shoulders and cheered.

"Bad Cat, Bad Cat, you're not as bad as all that!"

Then they threw a big block party. Everyone danced and laughed and joked and told their Bad Cat stories. Bad Cat started to sing again.

"They call me Bad Cat, Bad Cat, hooray, hip, hip, I can walk on my hands, I can do a backflip!"

HELP YOURSELF!

RIPE BANANAS

After all the excitement, Bad Cat felt tired. He waved to all his new friends and blew them kisses, and off he went.

Bad Cat stopped when he saw a little house. He jumped through the open window onto a big, comfortable bed. He started to bounce up and down, faster and higher. This was fun! *BOING! BOING! BOING!*

Suddenly a sleepy voice said, "Oh, you, bad cat! Stop that! Stop that!" It was Gloria the dancer, who had been asleep in her bed. Bad Cat bounced back out the window and down the street.

When Gloria saw the time she quickly hopped out of bed. "Oh, please come back!" she cried. "You woke me up! I would have been late for my evening show!"

But Bad Cat was far, far away.

"I'm Bad Cat, Bad Cat,
I'm on my way
to lots more adventures
in a new Big stinky day!

HA! HA! HA! HEY! HEY! HEY!"